# The Man with the Ice Blue Eyes

## Poems of Love and Heartache

# LISA G. SAMIA

proudly presented by
**DESTINY WHISPERS PUBLISHING, LLC**
TUCSON, ARIZONA
www.DestinyNovels.com

Author Copyright © 2016 by Destiny Whispers Publishing, LLC
LISA G. SAMIA, Author
THE MAN WITH THE ICE BLUE EYES / Destiny Whispers Publishing, LLC
Copyright © DESTINY WHISPERS PUBLISHING, LLC / June 30, 2016

**ISBN-13 # 978-1-943504-99-2**
**ISBN-10  # 1-943504-99-7**



Executive Editor: Leslie D. Stuart /.DestinyRose-Reads.com
Cover Art and Interior photography license:
BigStock Photos / www.bigstockphoto.com
Cover Art and Interior Graphic Designer:
LadyDestiny / Sr. Creative Director/ DWP, LLC
To request graphic art services please email Leslie D. Stuart at :
LadyDestinyAuthor@gmail.com



Destiny Whispers Publishing, LLC / Tucson, Arizona
AN EXTRAORDINARY JOURNEY ROMANCE NOVEL

www.DestinyNovels.com
www.DestinyAuthor.us
www.DestinyRose-Reads.com
www.LisaSamia.com

# Author Insights
# From Lisa G. Samia

"The Man with the Ice Blue Eyes" is a poetry collection
filled with love and heartache. A collection born
and felt of the deepest and most secret places of a
woman's heart. A place where only a woman could
understand the pain and the ecstasy of love, a place
we never speak about, yet we all know it exists.

How many of us in the throes of love have
knowingly sacrificed it all for that one look in his eyes,
the sight of his face, or the touch of his hand?

These heartfelt poems take you into this secret realm, a
place where only we as women would know what
we do for love; one taste of his kiss, to feel the longing
and ache that can only be quenched by him.

Read on and be swept away by love, and see if you
recognize the one man who could bend your knee,
the one who you dream of at night, who took your soul,
and opened your heart. For within ALL of us is
a part of a man that exists called
"The Man with the Ice Blue Eyes."

*For my husband Jim,*

*with love.*

*The one who*

*loves me the most,*

*and the one who*

*believes in me always*

# Dreams that Dance

I saw upon the dreams that danced
like Salome and love's last chance

and looked to see the heavenly hues
ribbons of violets, amber and blues

that left my heart
as begged to say
take me darling
take me away

for the clouds above
are such that it seems
floating laughter
passionate dreams

to take me beyond all that I care
the sight of you
and your ice blue stare.

# Drops of Love

The colored sky that made me weep
like drops of love from those who seek
and lay such gifts amongst the clouds
white, silent, serene and proud.

Of whose colors I had never seen
imperial, majestic that reign supreme
that capture my sight so as ever to see
the eyes beholden that bended my knee

And paint the sky the heavens above
with ribbons of beauty
passion and love
that take me beyond all I know
the sight of your eyes
that taunt me so.

# Reasons Why

that in all my spirits cease
to dream of dreams
in God's peace
and capture light...the summer sky
haunting and silent
without reasons or why...

and that so how it does seem
thoughts of love
laughter and dreams
that dance in clouds that bright the sky
ribbons of love that made me cry..

the heart that cries of love for you
to be touched and loved
painted in blue
like those eyes that taunt me no
my darling my life....I still love you so

# Ribbons of Blue

For all the times I saw those eyes
light ribbons of blue
under deep deep skies.

And watched them dance-glisten in dreams
like drops of love
cast from ancient means.

Be silent those eyes as I draw my stare
behold perfection so how I bear
those eyes that hold me forever and still
love, love you... always will.

# The Ice Cold Sky

The ice cold sky that began to melt
like frozen ice
or a heart so felt

Of colored blue in perfection it seems
of summer days
and sweet, sweet dreams

Of whom I see beyond the clouds
the eyes that haunt me
and cast me in shrouds

Of whose love I forever seek
past earth and sky
to take to meet.

# The Sight of Your Face

So how you know I love your face
the sight of it, does give me grace
Don't take it away for my eyes to see
that which gives me life to be.

Such beauty profound- silent and deep
eyes like heaven so they must weep
of the perfection given too just one
come my darling- we've just begun.

And fear not the love given so free
take my hand and you shall see
of how I love you deep within
my darling, my joy, my secret sin.

Forbidden as such yet taken away
tasted your lips yet did betray
of my care rejected it seems
living only within- on yesterday's dreams.

# Evening Hue

The evening sky painted pink and blue
a simple canvas of God's good hue
whose beauty is without name or grace
profound and silent
still in place.

That slowly slips from day to eve
perfection as only to easy to see
and lift one's eyes to that which is seen
a moment in life so pristine.

For which I think and pause to believe
a glimpse of heaven so perceived.
And hold my heart on bended knee
a place for me if only could be.

# Dear God

So then dear god what is wrong with me
that I have been so blind to see
of the wrong I did
and have begged to be free
of the grip of love that hold me fast
relentless, painful that did not last.

Please end these feelings I have inside
unrequited, not wanted...that cannot hide
from the look in his eyes
that haunts me so
wanting him close so how you know
that there is no care to come my way
begged and begged and did not stay.

So then god what shall I do?
Love is a gift...it comes from you
of this man I want to have heart
I love him, I love him so easy to part
and walked away so easy it seems
left me god, not even to dream.

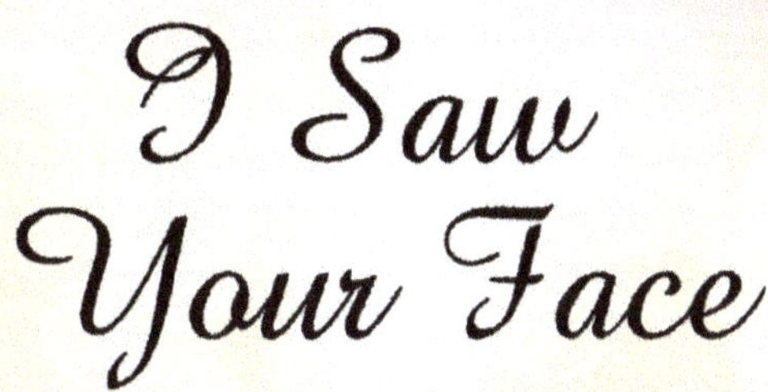

# I Saw Your Face

I saw your face in the morning hue
outlined in perfection so how I knew
the beauty as only God can provide
daydreams and laughter without care or pride.

That which I see in the dreamy light
your eyes magnificent - silent and bright
colored they are ice blue it seems
compelling they are destined to dream.

The face that haunts me as such this morn
broke my heart - left me forlorn
that lights this day to once again see
reminds me of you - if only could be.

# Dearest Lord

Dearest Lord hear my prayer
I ask your help
ease my despair
Of the feelings I have
for the one nearest to me
Help me dear Lord
I'm on bended knee.

And release me from this daily pain
of loving one who feels not the same
And forgive my discretion of bodies shared
never loved back and so never cared.

So dearest Lord I ask again
release me from the pain within
For with this burden I am not free
of the agony of the heart
that lives within me.

# Never Once Thought

Never once I thought it could ever be true
that I had loved you
so how you knew.

At such times when the pain was deep
wrenched my heart
beyond belief.

For a set of eyes that could melt the sky
and cause the strongest to be weak and die

All of which was so believed
love, laughter yet so deceived

The heart that proved so cold as ice
bottomless, frigid
of its own device.

No care nor love for me it seemed
left me lonely
for what it means.

# My Darling, My Love

I've cried for you many a day
wondered why you did not stay
and gaze at that which would not cease
an aching heart that longs for peace.

So then my darling what shall I do?
Tried to stop - from loving you
and so I fail each and every day
want you so much forever to stay.

I'm at my last - very last end
please love me back - please just bend
and take my body as once before
my heart you've had, forever and more.

For every day I am on bended knee
asking God to hear my plea
and take my hand unto your heart
and love me back - never to part.

And capture those eyes compelling in hue
resting beneath the softest of blue
and dream of days spent with me
my darling my love, if only you'd see.

# Glorious Gaze

The morning sun that cradled your face
in casted hues of God's good grace
and rested there for me to see
the love in your eyes if only for me.

Silently - the eyes - so blue
waking from sleep in glorious hue
of reflections of dreams in light and love
gifted if only as from above.

In wake and slumber they haunt my heart
compelling in beauty so as not to part
like frozen ice behind the sky
that make me weak and make me cry.

# Hasten to Me

When you go home - do you think of me?
and dream of moments that could be
and know that I do love you - so
hold me tight and don't let go.

For the fleeting dream could be so real
so I wait and deeply feel
for the moment when you give your hand
leave all behind - take that stand.

For I would never turn you away
give my love - forever to stay
and share my body, my heart, my dreams
with only you forever it seems.

Hasten now my darling - have no fear
for I will reach for you ever so near
and want you forever within my sight
hurry my darling - with all your might.

# I Remember the Day

So how then I remember the day
the first time you came my way
and glanced at me with eyes so true
colored they were like ice blue.

And in that moment frozen in time
only wanted you for mine
to have those eyes only want me
forsaking others if only to be.

And kiss those lips
in your haunting face
without ever caring in what place
or who should see or come what may
taking my heart forever to stay.

To this day I say again
I have loved you without end
and want you so until end of time
aching for you - please be mine

# I Still Miss You

I miss you so much so deep it seems
beyond my heart, past my dreams
of such a time when you came to me
rested and believed of which could be.

Of hidden lies I did not believe
could ever be so deeply deceived
So deep and painful the heart so mourned
used and left, such deep discord
for all I did was to tell of my care
why then such deep despair?

Yes in all I miss you still
beyond so, you never will
such a fool I never did see
the unkind you, so then it be.

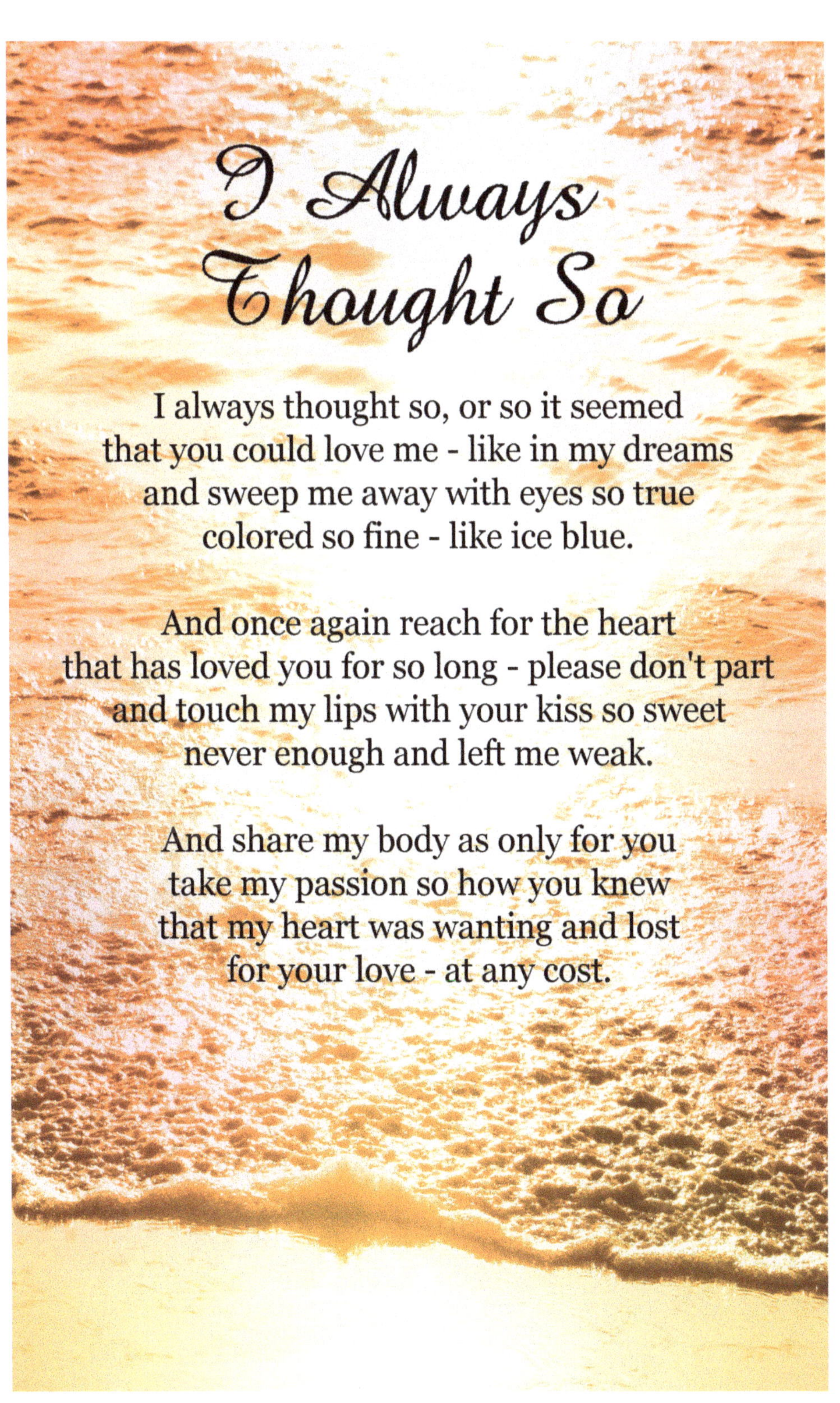

# I Always Thought So

I always thought so, or so it seemed
that you could love me - like in my dreams
and sweep me away with eyes so true
colored so fine - like ice blue.

And once again reach for the heart
that has loved you for so long - please don't part
and touch my lips with your kiss so sweet
never enough and left me weak.

And share my body as only for you
take my passion so how you knew
that my heart was wanting and lost
for your love - at any cost.

# The Fading Sky

The fading sky that drew me near
of nighttime hues that held me dear
of silent beauty that make me feel
of your eyes so deep - so real.

Of whose cast God must have seen
of perfection in nature so pristine
like frozen ice - behind the sky
colored blue that made me cry.

And of such passion for which I loved
ached for you - like a cooing dove
and still pine to once again see
the love in your eyes, if only for me

*** Winning Poem:
"The Fading Sky"
Connecticut Author's and Publisher's Writing Contest
Honorable Mention

# Dreams

The morning mist that touched my face
caressed it still in warm embrace
that reached for you to touch my heart
so keep asleep as not to part.

Laughter and breezes so fine and light
that danced through my dreams as only in night
saw your face so close so near
come my darling have no fear.

For love and care is within your reach
slumber so quiet sleep in peace
for I am there in your deepest dreams
I always will be – forever it seems.

*** *Winning Poem – "Dreams"*
*Connecticut Author's and Publisher's Writing Contest*
*First Place*

# I Guess I'm Ready

I guess I'm ready or so it seems
to let go of yesterday's dreams
to walk away from those ice blue eyes
that drove me mad and made me cry.

For all the time I waited to see
for you to come back and set me free
and I would have begged for the smallest crumb
from your ice cold table that made me numb.

So I guess I'm ready so now it seems
to leave you behind for what it means
It could be so much better, I said from the start
you never believed, so now to part.

# My Sweet Star

It never ceases to amaze me
never ceases to end
the eyes beholden that holds my heart
perfection in beauty so as not to part.

It never ceases to amaze me
never ceases to end
the face I yearn to see
desire within that haunts me so
deeply driven so how you know.

It never ceases to amaze me
never ceases to end
love unanswered for so long
that I so ache for all you are
sent from heaven, my sweet star.

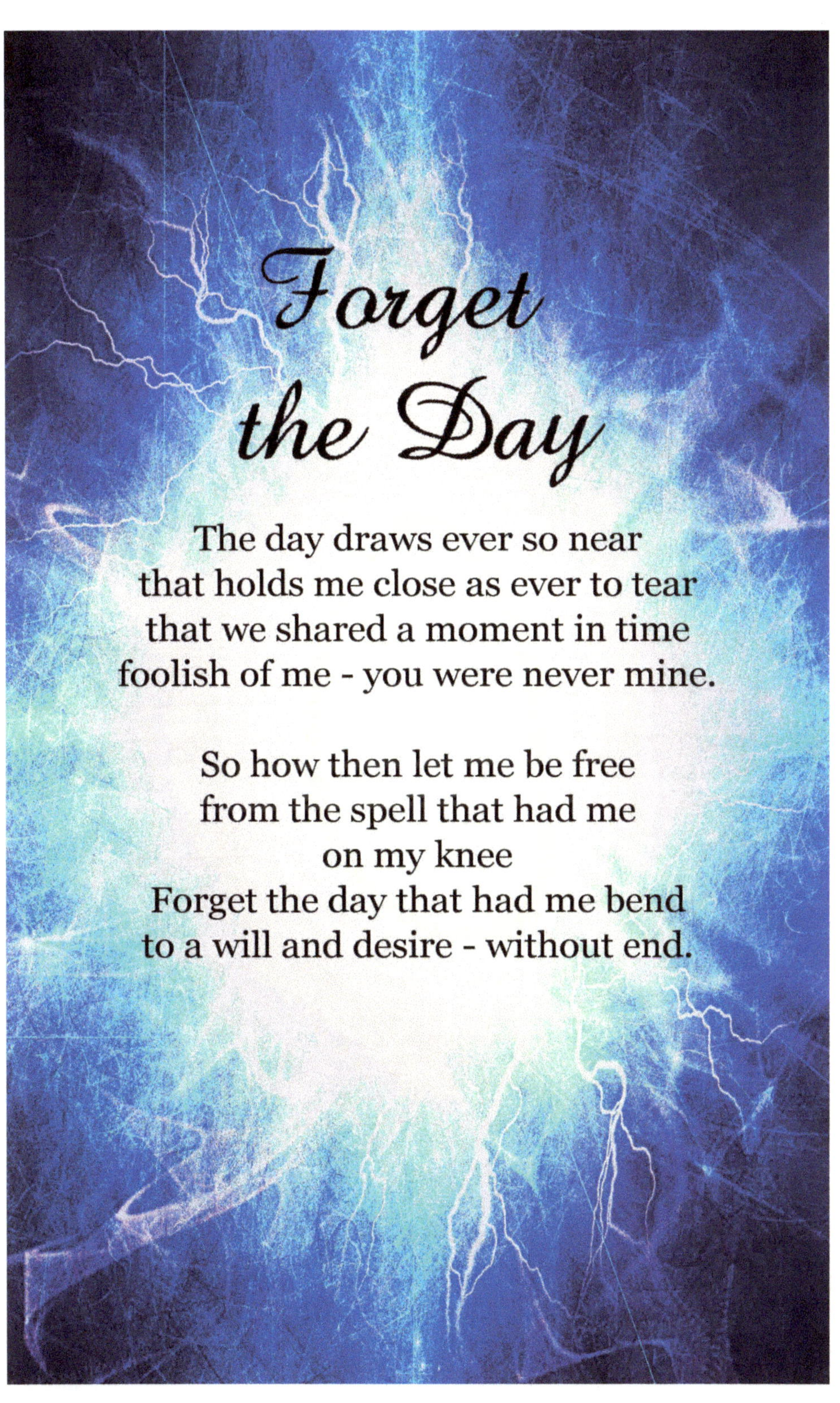

# Forget the Day

The day draws ever so near
that holds me close as ever to tear
that we shared a moment in time
foolish of me - you were never mine.

So how then let me be free
from the spell that had me
on my knee
Forget the day that had me bend
to a will and desire - without end.

# Deity Above

Help me deity above supreme
that rules with compassion or so it seems
and release my heart of its deepest pain
for now I implore your most sovereign reign.

For this man I see yet everyday
whose eyes beholden come what may
so how then I shared my heart
ache for him still did part.

Whose face draws me so ever near
and whispers promise ne'er to fear
and yet I still ache for him to say
come with me, let me take you away.

Such past delights that have left me in need
of your lips and desire on which to feed
and offer my body as proof of love
taken and used beyond and above.

So then deity above I am on my knees
bended before you so how I plead
release me from those eyes that have me blind
that have captured my soul and haunted my mind.

And let me walk away and never again think
of the man whose desire I did so wantonly seek
and let me rest from these feelings at last
and release me then from this prison past.

# Ever and Never a Time Ago

It was ever and never a time ago
or so it seemed to me
that you and I were together in love
albeit in a dream.

Dream swept days, white hot nights
whispered so fine and light
like cooing doves as one not two
as perfection in sky in flight.

It was or so it seemed to be
kisses so free and dear
upon waiting and wanting lips for you
left me you did in fear.

It was ever and never a time ago
your touch set my skin aflame
waiting for you to take my desire
my heart my soul to claim.

How then please so easily
you laughed and walked away so complete
when I still pine and cry for you
come back my love, my sweet.

So how then shall I ever go on
when all I want is you
to take my passion, my heart, my soul
yet played me for a fool.

# My Darling My Dream

Please understand my darling, my dream
that I must leave you my dear
for I cannot take being close to you
so driven it seems to tears.

Please understand my darling, my dream
the scent of you drives me weak
to always want you close to me
for those arms I long to seek.

Please understand my darling, my dream
your eyes are etched in my heart
to never see that face again
for never have I wanted to part.

Please understand my darling, my dream
your kiss has melted my soul
and burned the memory of desires beyond
all that time ago.

Please understand my darling, my dream
your body set my love aflame
carried me beyond the stars
left now yet only blame.

Please understand my darling, my dream
my desire to love you whole
and give you all that is of me
body, heart and soul.

Please understand my darling, my dream
that this truly must be goodbye
for I cannot have you again
left only then but to cry.

# So Then it Came to Be

So how then it came to be
vivid images of you and me
danced through my heart for you to see
kisses, embraces from I, to we.

Did not know please not to wake
having you close, so much at stake
your lips to taste to claim as mine
shared your body veiled desire as kind.

Wanted more then, now still do
crazy about you, so how you knew
keep asleep and dreams so fair
please not to wake left lost in despair.

So how then it came to be
was you to me in only a dream
see you now without your care
cannot touch you, still love not fair.

I know now it can never be
more than a fading glimpse that will never see
still that I love you from my heart
left unrequited never wanted to part.

Don't be afraid for I adore you so
your care is safe with me please know
that I will never abandon you in vain
and my heart will forever refrain.

"Come then let me take you away
to a place in the heart only you can stay
and forever live and love to my soul
come to me darling, I love you so".

# Foolish Dreams

Though I've made mistakes
too many to name,
and been forgiven many times the same,
yet still and all I wish to say
that I would leave you come what may
To save what is left of my grievous heart
then only for sure would then to part.

To find such peace on the other side
never to see you, embrace my pride
And maybe then only will I be whole,
body, mind and gentle soul.
Until then it does not cease,
relentless pursuit of elusive peace.

So yet I want to find my way
away from you never to stay
and never see your face again
the eyes beholden without end.
Such pain caused by your lack of care
has driven me into dark despair.

So deity above help me find my way
out of this darkness forever to say,
"that I will never want to see you again
nor think of you so easily when
and walk away without a thought it seems
and heal my foolish heart that believed in dreams"

# The Leaves that Fall

So how then I watch the leaves that fall
like manna from heaven that graced us all

And swirl about the earth with nowhere to go
as only God's breath can tell them so

And beg of you to open to see
that heart of yours that is not free

And let me in to fill your need
with all that I am and can ever be

So how then the earth now prepares to sleep
to go asunder and quietly weep

Open your heart please you can
for me to love, such a sweet dear man

# The Eyes that Haunt Me

The sight of your eyes so deep so blue
that brighten the sky with their changing hue
and called to my heart as if in a dream
the beauty that haunts me that reigns supreme

And take me away with your ice blue stare
matters not - ever - beyond compare
for the sight of those eyes will ever be
my fall from grace ne'er to see.

# Bitter Sweet

So if I thought of how to say good-by
like heaven above
that came and cried.

And leave you now as never to see
those ice blue eyes
that lowered my knee.

And say to you so as not to hear
laughter and love
and deep despair.

So as not to see you again
a piece of my heart
that does not mend.

And woe to me as I turn so complete
from all that I know
a taste of bitter sweet.

# I Miss You Darling, I Really Do

I miss you my darling I really do
The smile so sweet the eyes so blue
Of whom I have loved from the very first sight
Of the haunting eyes that wake my night

Of all that was for that moment in time
Captured my heart and tortured my mind
I've tried to let go but to no avail
I cannot stop yet continue to fail

For the nearness of you is like a dream
Fleeting yet beautiful yet somehow mean
I reach to touch and caress your face
Bowing me over falling from grace

What then is left for me?
Come to me or let me be
So I am on bended knee
To beg for a crumb and make you see

That I will wait forever and ever it seems
To once again kiss your face and dream my dream

# The Man with
# The Ice Blue Eyes

Of such time I thought I would never again see
the touch of your lips to mine could be
and never thought to hear you say
kiss me darlin' let me take you away.


So as you leaned so close so near
the scent of your being beyond my fear
and inhale the fragrance of your very soul
that leaned to me and melted like gold


So then how I caressed your face
the beauty of which felled my grace
and etched the sight of those ice blue eyes
the ones that haunt me and make me cry


And then see you ever so near
to kiss my lips with such care and dear
And left me wanting all the more
for the man I wait for, the man I adore.

If you enjoyed the carefully chosen pictures and the heartfelt words of this beautiful poetry collection, please kindly support the author's creative talents and leave a review on Amazon, Barnes & Noble, and GoodReads.

DESTINY WHISPERS PUBLISHING, LLC
www.DestinyNovels.com
www.DestinyAuthor.us

# About the Author

## Lisa G. Samia

Lisa G. Samia is an Award Winning Author who loves American History. She devoted three years travelling, researching and writing the fictional novel based on John Wilkes Booth *"My Name is John Singer."*

She graduated from the University of Massachusetts with a degree in English and has appeared on local television multiple times for her writing. A Boston native, she is happily married and lives in Avon, CT.

Lisa is also an accomplished poet. Her book "The Man with Ice Blue Eyes" which released July 2016, is a compelling collection of love poems that touch and pierce the heart. She is currently working on a sequel to "My Name is John Singer."

www.DestinyNovels.com
www.DestinyAuthor.us
www.LisaSamia.com

# ACCOMPLISHMENTS:

- Author of the extraordinary romance, "*My Name is John Singer*" a fictional second chance story based upon John Wilkes Booth
- Author of "*Don't Be Afraid of Fifty*," -- The Twelve Step Process to Turning Fifty.
- Appeared on CT-FOX 61 morning news program, WFSB Channel 3, Better CT and multiple times at WTNH Channel 8, Connecticut Style.
- Appeared on two Cable access channels; West Hartford, CT discussing "*Don't Be Afraid of Fifty*" and appeared in Guilford, CT discussing the award winning essay "*My Tiny Pieces of Wood*".
- Multiple book signings at Connecticut area Barnes and Noble's including Glastonbury, West Hartford and Canton and The Eastern States Exposition (The Big E) in Springfield, MA.
- Awards from the Connecticut Authors and Publishers Association Writing Contest 2013-2014 2nd place Essay and Honorable Mention Poetry; 2014-2015 1st place Poetry.

- Member of the following Historical Societies:
  - Ford's Theater, Washington, DC
  - Lincoln Cottage, Washington, DC
  - The Surratt Society, Clinton, MD
  - The Junius Brutus Booth Society (Tudor Hall), Bel Air, MD
- Graduate of University of Massachusetts Boston. Originally from Boston MA and currently resides in Avon, CT.

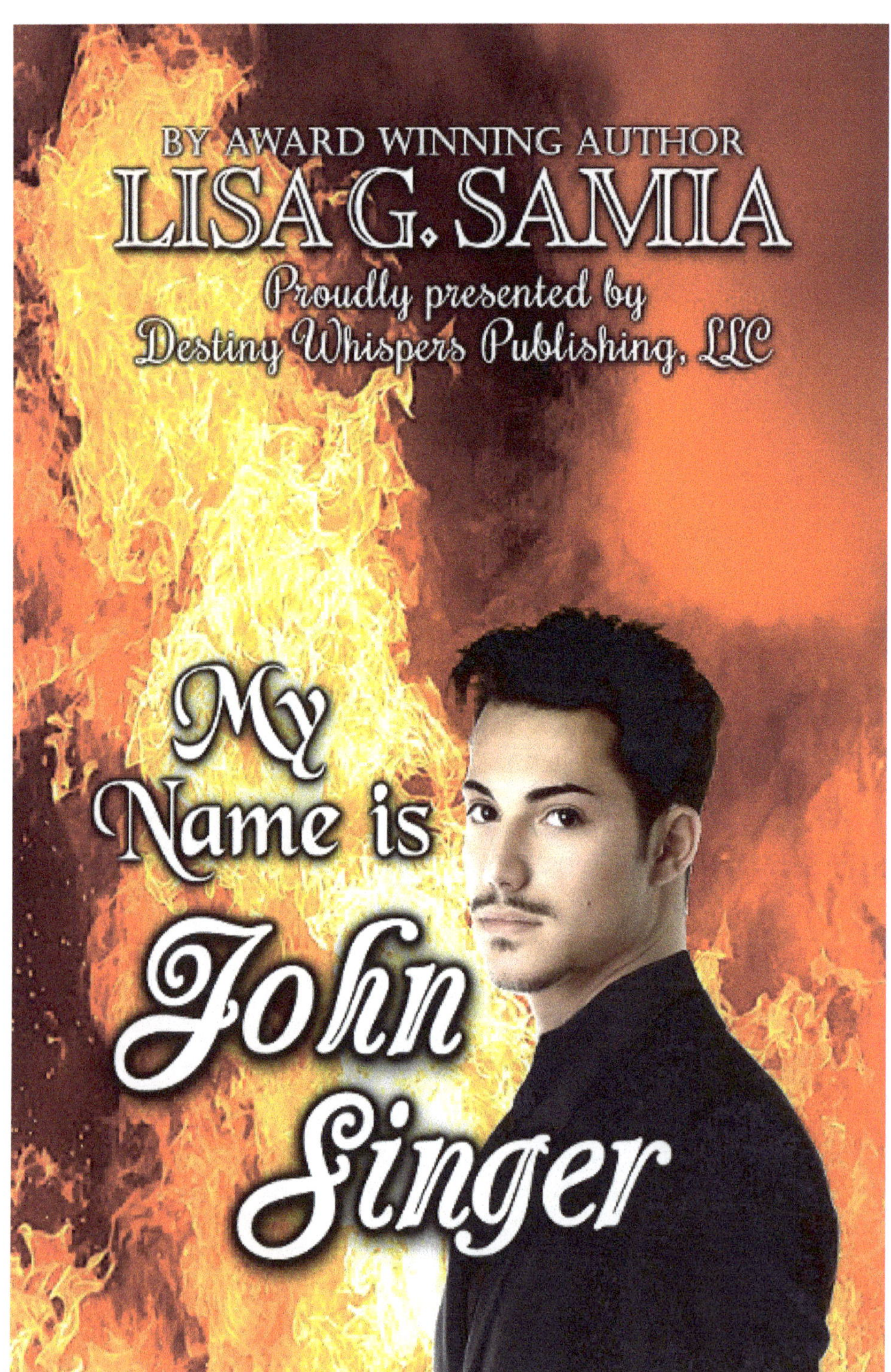

BY AWARD WINNING AUTHOR
LISA G. SAMIA
Proudly presented by
Destiny Whispers Publishing, LLC
My Name is John Singer

# ONLY LOVE COULD SAVE HIM

History tells us on April 26, 1865 a notorious assassin was cornered inside a burning barn, a Union gunshot ending his life. But rumors speculate he escaped that fiery blaze. Perhaps a twist of fate offered a second chance to right the wrongs and possibly find love.

When John Singer meets triage nurse, Emma Dixon at the war hospital in Alexandria, VA his body is broken, his spirit unwilling to fight as fever rages within him. But one smoldering glance from his black bottomless eyes, Emma knows he must survive. John's heart is stolen by her beauty and kindness. He is hiding in plain sight... or is he?

His true identity becomes his darkest secret. The world believes the blaze took his life. But John's tattered past still burns, scorching his mind with ashes of regret.

**For the handsome Confederate soldier known as John Singer is the notorious assassin JOHN WILKES BOOTH**

This compelling fictional account takes a bold look at the questionable possibilities swirling around Booth's enigmatic end, questions that still resonate today. The author romanticizes the complicated man, but never forgives his crimes. In this intriguing tale Booth is repentant.

*From the Author, Lisa G. Samia:*

*"In this fictional account I believed there was but one thing that could save him, and that was Love. For in the end, isn't Love all we have?"*

*Proudly presented by Destiny Whispers Publishing, LLC*
*www.DestinyNovels.com  - & -  www.DestinyAuthor.us*
*Executive Editing by Destiny Rose Editorial Services*
*www.DestinyRose-Reads.com*

ISBN#13- 978-1-943504-06-0
ISBN #10- 1-943504-06-7
$14.99 US / $16.99 CAN

# CHAPTER ONE
## *To survive war is to survive Hell.*
### *~~ Emma Dixon*

It was early May of 1865.

The young woman stood still, her blonde head slightly tipped to hear the field wagon approach on the uneven rutted roads that led to the hospital in Alexandria, Virginia. After working as a nurse here for three years, her ears were trained to listen for the signal that more men were coming who needed care and comfort.

During the war she had volunteered to serve, intending to do her part to help the Southern cause for only a few months, but the need for good medical staff was too great and the war lingered on for years.

Emma never left.

Releasing a heavy sigh as she watched the wagon coming into sight, exhaustion filled her heart. It would be another long day. Like every day since the war began, she endured endless hours at the hospital where the work to comfort and tend the wounded never felt complete. Endless days of watching men fall victim to the onslaught of brother against brother, friend against friend, and neighbor against neighbor in the American Civil War.

It broke her heart to hear stories of bravery and sacrifice whispered among the men staying here. Some tales were too heartbreaking to even repeat, stories Emma Dixon wished weren't true and she wanted to forget.

By all accounts of war news recently coming to them, the flow of wounded men would soon stop.

A Southern surrender had occurred. Just one month prior at Appomattox Courthouse, Virginia, numerous witnesses brought stories of how the Confederate leader General Robert E. Lee gave over to the Union army, surrendering his forces into the hands of General Ulysses S. Grant.

The Civil War had left a bloody path across the United States.

The slaves were free now.

The South had rejoined the Union.

The war was over, yet this General Hospital in Alexandria remained open to receive the last vestiges of the injured Confederate army. Men lay injured across the countryside. The wagons brought them in as the wounded were found in the nearby forests and fields, some barely clinging to life.

As the wagon pulled to the wooden emergency doors of the hospital and she saw other hospital staff hurry to carry the wounded men inside, Emma walked faster. Brushing back stray blonde strands near her cheeks and forehead that had come loose from the intricate knot pinned at the nape of her neck, she tidied her appearance.

She would be needed soon.

Here, a triage nurse might be a man's last chance.

Tonight she had the evening shift, from dusk until midnight, the hours when an injured man had nothing to do but suffer, sleep or die.

Exhaustion and responsibility weighed heavy upon her slim shoulders.

The past few weeks of the war had been especially trying.

The Confederate surrender was welcome news, meaning an end to the conflict and suffering, but fast on its heels came the shocking news of President Abraham Lincoln's murder on April 14th at Ford's Theater in Washington, D.C.

The assassination was conceived and carried out by a Confederate sympathizer. But Emma also knew the famous young actor, John Wilkes Booth had paid mightily for his crime, having been murdered himself twelve days later, on April 26, by Boston Corbett of the Sixteenth New York Cavalry.

Stories claimed the assassin was shot through the neck, much like the martyred President. Booth ran from the law after his deadly deed in the theater, but the Calvary finally trapped him at Garrett's tobacco barn near Port Royal, Virginia. His fellow conspirators were also caught and now sat in a Washington prison awaiting their fate.

A military trial could certainly lead them to the gallows.

So much death.

It wears down the hearts of the living.

Those grievous thoughts saddened her heart as Emma reached the front doors of the hospital and wandered into the central corridor.

The suffering here felt overwhelming today.

For a moment she stood against the well-worn wall and leaned her cheek against it, feeling coolness the early spring evening brought, knowing it was a prelude to the wet summer heat that would soon come.

A brigade of injured men streamed by her, some carried on stretchers, some hobbling on makeshift crutches. Most men were alone, but some were lucky enough to arrive with comrades who felt unwilling to leave their injured friend.

Triage in this field hospital did not always carry a successful outcome.

Emma dreaded the numerous amputated arms and legs that would soon litter the hospital surgery ward, then would be carried away in wagons and buried.

Another loss of war that changed lives.

As she entered the triage ward, Emma saw a previously empty bed was now occupied by the last man brought in by a hospital attendant.

He sat upright in a cot, his face stained with sweat and dirt, the Confederate gray uniform threadbare. The man's expression was tight with lips firmly pressed in silent repose. His casted leg was dirty from the earth and stained red with blood from a possible bullet wound.

It was a sight all too familiar to her war-weary eyes.

Giving the man a curt nod, her mind remained focused upon others with deeper immediate need.

Tonight the numbers of injured and sick men were many, with few nurses to offer aid. Emma yearned for the day when the broken men stopped arriving, for the night when the war, for her, would truly end.

She wove through the ward, stopping at various bedsides to change injury dressings, bring water, cool feverish faces and bodies, like she had done a thousand times before. The hands of men needing help and comfort were held out to her, all seeking a touch of kindness she so readily gave.

Hours had passed.

Evening had turned into a warm spring night.

Suddenly she felt a slight shiver as if being touched.

Emma turned slightly, feeling commanded to look. The sensation was eerie, a command without words, motion, or sound. Yet she felt it as real as the air inside her lungs and her heart that quickly beat beneath her breast.

Scanning across the hospital ward, her gaze suddenly stopped short.

Then she saw him again.

It was the man with the threadbare uniform, the one with the broken leg and possible bullet wound. He still wore a reticent composed face. He sat upright in his bed several rows away, his dark eyes fixed on her face.

The commanding power in them drew her.

He bore no smile. Yet it was compelling.

Emma met his bold stare, unable to turn away. She studied his face, now cleaned of the dirt and grime from earlier in the day.

Someone had shaved him. He was an average sized man with a lean, almost elegant form.

Those eyes captured her.

They were an unrelenting dark color like the depth of night, eyes that gave everything and promised nothing. That piercing gaze seemed to reach into the depths of her heart as if he knew the loneliness that had besieged her these three long years.

The boldness in their locked gaze should have felt uncomfortable.

She should have turned away.

Yet something warm stirred inside her heart, like recognition of something important and vital, bringing with it a strange and powerful attraction.

Emma had never known anything like this.

She lowered her emboldened gaze for a moment, but he still looked. The desire she felt from the man's eyes pulled her back to meet his stare without apology or regard for manners or decorum.

The corners of her lips curved, ever so slightly.

She was entranced, powerless to stop.

In answer, his brow arched, in a question and nearly a challenge.

Without any words or a single touch, Emma knew the man found her beautiful. It was flattering, but this handsome man was certainly not the first to look at her with lust in his eyes.

The good Doctor Bradley, the young and talented physician did it all the time.

But the young physician never made her heart race nor had the natural born charisma that made all other attractive men seem rough and unpolished, in comparison.

This man was different. Special.

She saw his left leg was recast and his wound re-bandaged. Emma hoped if it was a bullet that caused the blood stain she saw earlier, that it passed through soft flesh, not tearing through and splintering bones causing internal injuries that assured a slow and painful death.

If it didn't heal, the swift knife of the surgeon was the only other remedy.

The thought of this extraordinary man amputated with only one leg to work with, to love with, was incredulous to her.

One last time, she met his gaze again. The man was impossible to ignore. The urge to go to him was nearly irresistible.

Yet, she did resist.

Determined to remain in control, Emma lifted her chin a little and across the sea of wounded men, she stood firm.

He never said a word, yet she sensed the power of his will, drawing her into his world.

For long moments, only he and she seemed to exist.

Soon the quiet cries of injured men needing comfort and care moved Emma to continue her work. But with each bedside she visited that night, his intense dark gaze followed her, silent and compelling.

**********

*We hope you enjoyed the excerpt from*

*"My Name is John Singer"*

His eyes followed her as she worked.
Black, bottomless and compelling, unmatched and
unforgettable. Nothing in Emma's life prepared her to
meet those eyes, the eyes of the handsome confederate
soldier known as John Singer.

**Available worldwide in all EBook formats for
digital readers and beautiful printed books.
Sold on Amazon, Barnes & Noble, Kobo,
Smashwords, and at all fine book retailers.**

**Look for Lisa's exciting sequel to
"My Name is John Singer," to find out what
happens to John and Emma.**